Fast Break

Bob Wright

High Noon Books
Novato, California

Cover Design: Jill Zwicky
Interior Illustrations: Ke Sneller

International Standard Book Number: 0-87879-990-7

10 09 08 07 06 05 04 03
15 14 13 12 11 10 9 8 7

You'll enjoy all the High Noon Books.
Write for a free full list of titles.

Contents

CHAPTER 1

Lions vs. Mustangs

The ball rested on the rim for a second. It didn't fall through the basket. And it didn't roll off the rim.

There were two hundred fans in the gym. There were cheerleaders for both teams. Everyone was screaming. The coaches looked at the clock. There were five seconds left in the game. The score was 79 to 79.

The Jackson Lions wore the red jerseys. The Washington Mustangs wore the blue jerseys.

Suddenly the ball moved. It rolled off the rim.

Deke yelled, "Now, Kelly!"

Kelly didn't even look at the ball. He began to run to the other end of the court.

Deke jumped for the ball. He jumped as high as he could. He grabbed the ball. He couldn't see Kelly. He had his back to him. But Deke knew where Kelly was.

This was their best play. It was called the "fast break." With both hands Deke threw the ball way over his head. The ball flew to the other end of the court. No one was there except Kelly.

There were three seconds left in the game. Kelly had an easy shot. He smiled before he took the shot. He yelled back at Deke, "Thank you, Deke."

Both teams were rushing down the court toward Kelly. Deke screamed at Kelly, "Shoot the ball, Kelly! Please! Shoot!"

Kelly was still smiling. Deke couldn't believe it. But he had to laugh. Some of the fans were laughing. The cheerleaders were screaming. Finally Kelly shot the ball. There was one second left.

The ball hit the backboard and went right through the basket. The game was over. The Lions had beat the Mustangs by the score of 81 to 79.

"How did you like my great shot?" Kelly asked Deke in the locker room.

Deke put his arm around Kelly. "The shot was OK. But what about my great pass?"

Kelly pushed Deke away and laughed. He

started to say something to Deke. But the coach came and stood between Kelly and Deke. The coach was mad. His face was as red as a tomato. He grabbed Kelly by the arm. He shouted, "What were you doing out there?"

Kelly tried to pull his arm away from the coach. "I was out there playing basketball," he said.

The coach said, "You are a hot dog. Do you know what a hot dog is?"

Kelly smiled at Deke. Then he said to the coach, "Sure. A hot dog is something to eat for lunch."

The coach shouted at Kelly, "A hot dog is a show-off!"

Deke cut in. "Aw, coach, take it easy. We won

The coach said, "You are a hot dog!"

the game. That's what counts."

"Stay out of this, Deke," the coach said. "If Kelly does that again, I will put him on the bench."

The coach walked away. Kelly pulled off his red jersey and tossed it into his locker. He was mad.

CHAPTER 2

The Hero

Deke and Kelly left the locker room together. They walked side by side. But no one said a word. Deke was waiting for Kelly to say something first.

Finally Kelly said, "The coach is nuts."

Deke said, "Aw, the coach is OK. He just gets upset."

They walked over to Bill's Cafe. They went in to get a Coke. They sat at the counter.

Deke said, "You should have shot the ball

right away, Kelly. You shouldn't have smiled. You shouldn't have yelled to me. There were only three seconds left."

"But I thought it was funny," Kelly said.

"It was funny to me, too," said Deke. "But not to the coach. He gets too upset."

Kelly was going to say something. But then two cheerleaders came into Bill's Cafe. One of the cheerleaders was Sue. Kelly liked her a lot. The other was Mary. Deke liked her. Sue waved to Kelly, and Mary smiled at Deke. The two girls walked over to the counter. "You guys were great," Sue said.

Kelly laughed. "We know we're great, don't we, Deke?"

Deke just smiled. He was looking at Mary. But he didn't want her to know he was looking at her.

Sue said to Kelly, "It was so cool when you yelled at Deke before you shot the ball. I've never seen anything like that before."

Kelly turned to Deke. "See? I told you that was funny."

Deke just smiled again. He was still checking out Mary. Soon the rest of the team came into Bill's. A boy named Willie hit Kelly on the arm and said, "You were the hero. You won the game. Who do we play next week?"

"The Tigers," Kelly said. "Isn't that right, Deke?"

Kelly knew that Deke was checking out Mary. He knew that Deke didn't hear a word. Suddenly Deke turned around and said, "Wh. . . What?"

Kelly laughed. Deke's face turned red. Kelly said, "We play the Tigers next week. And we'll give them the same treatment we gave the Mustangs."

"That's right," Willie said. And everyone laughed.

CHAPTER 3

Lions vs. Tigers

The first half of the game was almost over. The Lions were leading the Tigers 33 to 27. Both Deke and Kelly had played well. The coach watched Kelly very closely.

Suddenly Deke grabbed a loose ball. He yelled, "Now, Kelly!" They were going to do a fast break. Deke threw the ball as far as he could. Kelly was standing under the basket. He caught the ball.

There were no Tigers near Kelly. He had an

easy shot. But he didn't shoot right away. He stuck the ball between his legs. And then he looked at the cheerleaders. He looked at Sue. Then he bowed to her. Everybody in the gym laughed except the coach.

Now Kelly was going to shoot. He reached down for the ball. But he was too late. One of the Tigers came up behind him. He poked at the ball. The ball bounced away from Kelly. Another Tiger picked it up and threw a long pass. The Tigers scored a basket just before the first half ended.

The locker room was as quiet as a graveyard. Kelly sat in front of his locker and looked at the floor. Deke sat next to him.

The coach walked into the locker room. He walked over to Kelly. He said, "You are the best shooter on the team. But you would rather be a movie star than a ball player. I don't need movie stars on this team. I need ball players. If we beat the Tigers today, we will play the Larks next week. If we beat the Larks, we will play the Bears. If we beat the Bears, we will be the champs. So you see, I need ball players."

Kelly looked up at the coach. "I'm a ball player. We'll go out there now and beat the Tigers bad."

The coach said, "You're not going anywhere. You will sit on the bench for the rest of the game. You will sit on the bench until you tell me that you are sorry."

Kelly said nothing. Deke poked Kelly in the ribs. "Say you're sorry. Get it over with."

Kelly said nothing. The coach walked away. The whole team was looking at Kelly. Deke said, "Come on, Kelly. Just say that you're sorry."

Kelly wouldn't look at Deke. He looked at the floor and said, "I'm not sorry." Then he took off his jersey and grabbed his towel from the locker. He went straight to the showers.

In the second half, the Lions did not play well. Deke threw long passes to Willie and to Joe. But they were not as fast as Kelly. The fast break was not working. Deke was sure they were going to lose. But they didn't. The Tigers were having a bad day. And the Lions won 58 to 55.

After the game Deke looked around the gym for Kelly. He couldn't find him. He looked in the locker room. Kelly wasn't there. No one had seen Kelly.

CHAPTER 4

Kelly and the Gambler

When Kelly left the gym, he rode the bus downtown. He didn't want to see anyone from the team. He went into the pool hall.

"What's doing, hot shot?" asked Johnny-One-Eye. Johnny was the man in charge of the pool tables.

"I'm doing OK," said Kelly.

"I thought you had a game today against the Tigers," said Johnny.

"Give me a Coke," Kelly said to Johnny.

"The team had a game today but I didn't. I'm not on the team any more."

"Since when?" asked a fat man with a cane.

Kelly didn't know who the fat man was. He had never seen him before. He didn't like his looks.

"Since when?" asked the fat man again.

Kelly looked at his Coke. He tried to ignore the fat man. The man came and stood next to Kelly. He stuck his fat face close to Kelly's face. "I asked you a question," he said.

Johnny-One-Eye said to Kelly, "You better answer Mr. Travis. He is a very important man."

Kelly looked at Mr. Travis. "I just quit the team today."

The fat man stood there. He tapped at his shoe with his cane. For a long time he didn't say anything. Then he asked, "Why?"

"I don't get along with the coach," Kelly told the fat man.

"That's very upsetting," the man said.

"It's no big deal," Kelly said.

"Maybe it's no big deal to you, kid. But I don't care about you. The person I care about is ME!"

Kelly sipped his Coke. "I don't know what you're talking about."

"Listen, kid. You don't know me. But I know you. If the Lions beat the Larks next week, I win two thousand bucks. If the Lions lose, I lose. Do you get what I'm saying?"

"I guess so," Kelly said in a low voice.

"What do you have to do to get back on the team?" the fat man asked.

"I have to tell the coach I'm sorry for showing off. But I won't do it. I won't say I'm sorry."

"Don't be a jerk," the fat gambler told Kelly. "Here's what I'm going to do. I'm going to give you one hundred dollars. You take the money. You keep it. It's yours. You just be sure to tell the coach you're sorry. I want you in that game against the Larks.

Kelly stared at him. "You mean you're going to give me a hundred dollars?"

"That's right, kid. Here it is right here. Put out your hand." The gambler counted out five twenty dollar bills. He put the money in Kelly's hand. "But you have to promise to tell the coach you're sorry."

Kelly said, "I promise, I promise. And thanks for the money."

The gambler said, "Yeah, sure, kid."

Kelly was very happy when he left the pool hall. He was rich! The gambler seemed to be a nice guy. But Kelly still didn't like him. He didn't know why.

CHAPTER 5

Kelly Is Rich

Kelly rolled up the five twenty dollar bills. He put the roll in his pocket. He walked down the street with his hand in his pocket. He kept feeling the money. He didn't want to lose it. Just then he saw Willy. Willy was riding his bike. He waved to Kelly. Kelly took his hand out of his pocket. He waved at Willie. The money fell out. It was blowing in the wind.

Kelly yelled, "Oh, no!" He chased after the money. He picked up four of the bills. But one of the bills blew under a car. Kelly got down on his hands and knees. He crawled under the car. He grabbed the bill. He crawled out. He stood up. He was very dirty now. There was oil all over his shirt and pants. He rolled up the money again. He put it back into his pocket. He said to himself, "I'll never wave to anybody again!"

Kelly was standing in front of a store. The name of the store was **Shoes, Shoes, Shoes**. Kelly went in.

The man in the store asked Kelly, "Can I help you?"

Kelly said, "I want to buy Michael Jordan shoes. I want to buy two pairs." Kelly wanted to buy shoes for himself and for Deke.

The man said, "That will cost two hundred dollars."

Kelly said, "Wow! I only have *one* hundred dollars."

The man laughed. He said, "You can buy a left shoe for yourself. You can buy a right shoe for your friend."

Kelly didn't laugh. He left the store. He took the money home and hid it in a small box in his closet.

The phone rang. It was Deke. "Hey, Kelly. I've been looking all over for you. Where have you been?"

Kelly said, "Oh, I've been here and there. I've been thinking."

"Thinking what?"

"I'm going to tell the coach that I'm sorry," said Kelly.

"Great," Deke said. "I'll meet you at the gym in ten minutes."

When Kelly got to the gym, he found Deke. Deke said, "Let's go see the coach." They knocked on the office door.

"Come in. The door's open," said the coach. Kelly and Deke went in.

Kelly said, "Coach, I've come to say that I'm sorry. I want to be back on the team."

"He really is very, very sorry," Deke said.

The coach looked at the two boys. He said, "Well, OK." And then he asked, "You won't pull any more movie star stuff?"

"No more," said Kelly.

"Well, OK," said the coach.

Kelly and Deke grinned at one another. They would be playing together again. No one could beat them now!

CHAPTER 6

Lions vs. Larks

The Lions had to beat the Larks. If they beat the Larks, they would play the Bears next week. If they beat the Bears, the Lions would be the champs.

The Larks took the first shot. The ball missed the hoop. Deke grabbed the ball. He yelled, "Kelly!"

Kelly started to run down the court. Deke threw a long pass. Kelly caught the ball. He took an easy shot. He missed.

In the first half of the game, Kelly missed five easy shots. The Larks were leading 25 to 20. The coach said to Kelly, "What's the matter? Why are you missing those easy shots?"

Kelly didn't know what was wrong. But Deke said, "I know what's wrong. You're trying too hard. You have to relax."

Deke was right. Kelly was afraid that the gambler would take back the hundred dollars. He didn't want to lose the money. He had to forget about the money.

Kelly was great in the second half. He took short shots and made them. He took long shots and made them. He stole the ball from the Larks. He passed the ball behind his back. He

In the first half of the game
Kelly missed five easy shots.

bounced the ball between his legs.

Some of the fans wanted Kelly to do something funny. They wanted him to bow to the cheerleaders. But tonight Kelly was not a movie star. He was a ball player.

There was one minute left in the game. The score was Lions 52, Larks 40. Everyone knew that the Lions would win.

Then Kelly saw the fat gambler. He was standing near the door of the gym and smiling. Kelly was sorry to see the gambler. And he was sorry he had ever taken the money from this Mr. Travis.

Kelly was trying to think and to play ball at the same time. He went up for an easy shot. And he missed. But it didn't matter. The game was over. The Lions had won.

In the locker room Deke said, "You were great today, Kelly. But that last shot was wild."

Kelly said, "I know. I was trying too hard again."

"Forget it," Deke said. "Let's ask Mary and Sue if they want to go out. We can go to Bill's for a burger."

CHAPTER 7

The Return of the Gambler

Deke, Kelly, Sue, and Mary went to Bill's. They sat at a table in the corner. Deke and Kelly sat on one side of the table. Mary and Sue sat on the other. Deke tried to think of something to say to Mary. But when Mary was around, he didn't know what to say. He thought he sounded stupid. So he didn't say much at all.

Kelly was just about to take a bite of his burger. Just then he saw someone at the front door. "Oh, no," he said.

Deke looked at Kelly. Then he looked at the door. He said to Kelly, "What's wrong? Who is that fat man with the cane?"

Sue said, "What's the matter, Kelly?"

The gambler walked over to their table. He looked down at Kelly. He said, "What's doing, kid?"

Kelly put down his burger. He said, "Hello, Mr. Travis."

The fat gambler said, "You don't look happy to see me, hot shot."

Kelly looked down at his burger. "I am here with friends," he said.

Mr. Travis tapped at his shoe with his cane.

"You don't look happy to see me, hot shot."

He smiled. He looked like a snake. He said to Kelly, "I am your best friend, hot shot. And don't you forget that."

Deke didn't like the way this fat guy was talking to Kelly. He started to say something. But Mary touched his hand. She wanted him to stay out of it. She could tell that the gambler was no good.

Then Mr. Travis said, "I want to talk to you and Deke. Tell the little girls here to take a walk."

This was too much for Deke. He was mad. He said to the gambler, "Why don't you take a walk? The girls will stay right here."

Kelly said, "Take it easy, Deke. Then he

turned to Mary and Sue. "Will you leave us alone for a few minutes?"

Sue was mad. Mary said to Deke in a low voice, "Be careful." And then the girls left.

The gambler said to Kelly, "You did fine today. I won my bet."

Kelly didn't say a word. Deke didn't know what was going on.

The gambler said, "Now I can make you both very rich. Next week you play the Bears. I made a bet that the Bears will win. I bet ten thousand dollars that the Bears will beat the Lions."

Kelly said, "What?"

"That's right," said the fat man. "I bet on

the Bears. You boys make sure I win that bet and I will make you rich. I will give you five hundred dollars each."

Kelly stared at him. "You mean you want us to try to lose the game? You want us to let the Bears beat us?"

"That's right, hot shot."

Deke said, "You must have a screw loose."

The gambler stood up. "I will meet you here after the game. Then I will give you the money."

CHAPTER 8

Lions vs. Bears

Kelly told Deke about the hundred dollars. "I thought it was OK. I thought he wanted the Lions to win all the games. Now he wants us to lose."

"It's all wrong," said Deke.

Kelly nodded his head. "I know."

"That guy is a crook," Deke said.

Kelly said, "I know that now. But what should we do?"

Deke said, "First, let's take that hundred

dollars to the coach. We'll tell him the whole story. He'll know what to do."

––––––––––––––––––––

Next week was the game against the Bears. The winner would be the champ. The gym was packed with screaming fans. The band played. The cheerleaders danced. The teams were taking warm-up shots.

One fan said, "There's Kelly. He's the best."

Another fan said, "There's Deke. I think he's the best."

At the end of the first quarter, the Bears were leading by a score of 17 to 15. In the second quarter, Deke and Kelly tried the fast break. Kelly put the ball through the hoop. And the score was tied.

Then the Bears tried a long pass. But Deke was there to get the ball. He threw it to Willie. Willie passed it to Sam, Sam passed it back to Willie. Willie threw it to Joe, and Joe made the basket. The Lions were ahead by two points.

The Bears were ahead in the fourth quarter, 50 to 47. Deke was fouled. He went to the foul line. And then he saw the gambler. Mr. Travis was sitting in the front row. He was smiling. He acted sure that Deke and Kelly would let the Bears win.

Deke called time-out. He walked over to Kelly. Deke said, "There's Mr. Travis over there. He's laughing. He thinks we're going to lose. We've got to win, Kelly."

Kelly said, "Don't worry, Deke. You make these two foul shots. And we'll wipe that smile off the fat man's face."

Deke made both shots. The score was Bears 50, Lions 49. And then Kelly went into high gear. The Bears never knew what hit them.

Kelly was all over the place. He took a long shot and made it. He took three short shots and made them all. He passed the ball to Sam. Sam shot and scored. Kelly passed the ball to Deke. Deke scored, Willie shot and missed. But Deke got the ball. He threw it to Kelly. Kelly faked a pass to Joe. But he threw the ball back to Willie. And this time Willie hit the mark.

Deke and Kelly did the fast break three times in a row. Kelly scored a basket each time.

There was a minute left in the game. The Lions were beating the Bears by a score of 69 to 55. The fans went wild. They knew that the Lions were now the champs.

CHAPTER 9

The Last Minute

The Bears called a time-out. Kelly walked over to Deke and said, "Look over there. Look at the fat man."

Deke looked at Mr. Travis. He was not smiling now. He just sat there in the front row. He was hitting his foot with his cane. He looked very sad and very mad at the same time.

Suddenly the fat man's face turned white. The gambler was looking over at the coach. The gambler stood up. He began to run up the stairs of the gym.

Deke and Kelly looked over at the coach. He was talking to two cops and pointing to the fat man.

The time-out was over. The game was just about to start again. The ref was standing down at the other end of the gym. The ref was holding the ball. Deke ran up to the ref and grabbed the ball. He yelled, "Kelly!" It was just like the fast break. Kelly ran to the bottom of the stairs. The fat gambler was almost at the top of the stairs. Deke threw the ball as hard as he could. Kelly caught it. And now Kelly threw the ball as hard as *he* could. The ball hit the fat man in the back of the head. The gambler went down. He tried to get up again but he slipped. And then he began to roll down the stairs. At the bottom the two cops grabbed him. Then they took him away.

The coach said, "You two really are champs. Now go and take your showers. And you better hurry. There are two fans over there waiting for you."

Deke and Kelly saw Mary and Sue standing at the door. The girls were smiling. Deke yelled, "Kelly!" Both boys ran to the showers as fast as they could.